Published exclusively for J Sainsbury plc
Stamford Street London SE1 9LL
by Walker Books Ltd
87 Vauxhall Walk London SE11 5HJ

First published 1991

First printed 1991
Printed in Hong Kong

ISBN 0-7445-1673-0

MY GRANDPA IS
AMAZING

Nick Butterworth

SAINSBURY · WALKER BOOKS

My grandpa is amazing.

He builds fantastic
sand-castles…

and he makes
marvellous drinks…

and he's not at all
afraid of heights…

and he makes wonderful
flower arrangements…

and he's a brilliant
driver...

and he knows
all about first aid...

and he's got
an amazing bike…

and he's a terrific dancer…

and he's very, very,
very patient…

and he invents
brilliant games.

It's great to have
a grandpa like mine.

He's amazing!